HENRY HUBBLE'S
BOOK OF TROUBLES

HENRY HUBBLE'S BOOK OF TROUBLES

ANDY MYER

A YEARLING BOOK

Copyright © 2015 by Andy Myer

All rights reserved. Published in the United States by Yearling, an imprint of Random House Children's Books, a division of Penguin Random House LLC, New York. Originally published in hardcover in the United States by Delacorte Press, an imprint of Random House Children's Books, New York, in 2015.

Yearling and the jumping horse design are registered trademarks of Penguin Random House LLC.

Visit us on the Web! randomhousekids.com

Educators and librarians, for a variety of teaching tools, visit us at RHTeachersLibrarians.com

Library of Congress Cataloging-in-Publication Data is available upon request.

ISBN 978-0-385-74440-9 (pbk.)

Printed in the United States of America
10 9 8 7 6 5 4 3 2 1
First Yearling Edition 2016

To Sandi, for her love and support and
for thirty-six years of priceless stories about
the students at Paul Fly Elementary School

If You're Reading This Journal . . .

Nuts! I guess I must've left it somewhere. Could have been the library, or maybe the ComixShop (I'm there a lot!). Or maybe you found it somewhere in my school, Orville Crumb (done laughing?) Middle School.

Well, who cares! The main thing is

YOU FOUND IT!!!

If it isn't too much trouble, could you please send it back to me, Henry Harrison Hubble? I'd really appreciate it, because there's some pretty personal stuff in here that I wouldn't want to get out. EVER!!

1

FYI, I'm named after William Henry Harrison, the ninth president of the United States. Nobody talks much about President Harrison, because he died 32 days after he became president. Pretty sucky luck, huh?

But guess what? My great-great-great-great-grandmother Ida Rosabelle Hubble lived RIGHT NEXT DOOR to him in Ohio when he was a senator. His dog, Jupiter, would come over all the time and drop his poop in her yard. Dad says we still have a dried-up dog-log in an old bottle in the attic, which I'm pretty sure must be worth a whole bunch of money.

I went on our computer and searched for "historic dog turds" to see how much it was worth. I only found one thing that said that in the Middle Ages you might be PAID in dog poop, and that people used it to CURE BALDNESS! If you ask me, I'd rather be bald than have my head covered in dog poop, but there probably weren't a lot of hair care products to choose from back then.

I guess there's really nothing I can do to stop you from reading this, if you're a nosy type of person. So if you're gonna read it, you might as well know that I keep VERY careful notes and drawings about my life. This is because I'm going to be a GREAT cartoonist someday.

Actually, I'd rather be one of those lucky guys that make cartoons, but every time I hear about a movie like *Toy Story 3*, it's something about how it cost millions and millions of dollars to make. Seeing as I'm only eleven, I don't have much money at any one time. Right now, I've only got $39 in a shoe box on the top shelf of my closet. So I don't see how I can make movies anytime soon.

Cartoonists really only need a Sharpie and some paper, which are pretty cheap and easy to find at places like Walmart and Staples. (Hey! I wonder if they'd pay me for mentioning them in my journal.) So I think this is a pretty smart career decision.

You'll also find that I write mostly about things that are going wrong in my life, which seems to be a lot, for some reason I can't explain. So most things are called some type of Trouble, one way or another.

Once in a while, something good happens, which I'll also include, just to be fair.

I guess one last thing I should explain is that I write poetry, too. I'm going to be the next Shel Silverstein, that bald guy who wrote all those funny poems. I guess if he'd lived in the Middle Ages, he'd be one of those guys who wore dog poop on his head.

I found out his real name was Sheldon, but I guess he thought that sounded too dorky, so he changed it. I don't blame him. I have the same problem with MY name. Maybe I'll call myself Hen Hubble.

I think poetry is the best way to say a lot with just a few words. So this also saves on my Sharpie and paper expenses.

Oh, snap!! I almost forgot to include my address so you can send this back to me. I'm at 54 Loon Road, Crumb Hollow, Pennsylvania. It's a yellow house with green shutters and a mailbox that I painted to look like President Harrison. You can leave my journal in there if I'm not home.

Henry H. Hubble
Book Bag Troubles

I am Henry Harrison Hubble.
My book bag gives me all kinds of trouble.
It's so darn heavy it hurts my knees.
It makes me sweat, stagger, and wheeze.

I'm starting with my book bag because really, most of my Troubles are in there, one way or another.

For starters, it's REALLY heavy, because I only put stuff in and never take anything out. This morning, though, I decided—for the first time since we bought it four months ago—to dump it out.

Here's what was inside:

- *American Vistas* (textbook)—two pounds
- *Adventures in Geometry* (textbook)—one pound
- *Our Universe* (textbook)—two pounds
- *The Red Badge of Courage* (boring novel)—just a quarter pound, but if you've ever read it you know it seems WAY heavier

So we're almost at six pounds already!
But wait, there's A LOT more. . . .

- Dried-up snakeskin. I use this about twice a week for changing the conversation when some big nasty kid asks me why I'm such a dweeb.
- Dried worms. They're great for spooking my dopey older sister, Haley.

I put a dried worm in Haley's cereal after she told Mom and Dad that I broke a vase in the living room (I was seeing if I could throw a Frisbee from the family room in the back of the house all the way to the front hall in one throw). Serves her right for being a SNITCH!!

- This is the remote for our TV in the den. Not really sure how this got in my bag. We looked for this for a WHOLE month, until my dad gave up and bought a new one—one of those univer-sal kinds that no one seems to know how to work. I don't think I'll say anything. I'll wait till we lose Mr. Universal, then just happen to find this one in Haley's room.

- Oh, boy! I've been looking for this! I was supposed to hand in this report on President Harrison last Friday. It's called "President Harrison: 31 Days of Glory." I had gobs of trouble making it to 150 words, but then I added how we have a bottle of poop from his dog, Jupiter, which made the total 149. Hopefully, my English teacher Mrs. Claster won't notice the missing word!

- This is my Red Sloth ring. I bought it used at a comic book store for $1.69, plus tax. Not many people  know about the Red Sloth. His main superpower is that he can hang in one spot indefinitely without moving. If he sees a crime taking place, he slowly creeps over the bad guys, points at them, and makes

9

fun of them until they get so angry and upset, they give up and leave. When he's not the Red Sloth, he's Walter Nagle, the mayor of Hinkleton, Wisconsin. Lots of people think the Red Sloth is the world's most boring superhero, but that's okay with yours truly.

- **Oh, brother!** This is a slip for a field trip we're taking in a couple weeks to look at some whales. I watch this show *Fish Tales* about this fleet of ships that go out every year in the Gulf of Mexico to catch anchovies that they make BIG money selling to pizza parlors. Sailors are washed overboard all the time!

- That slip is stapled to our school lunch menu, which our HORRIBLE cafeteria lady, Miss Vanderbeek, sends home every week. Believe me, the food doesn't make your mouth water. It's usually your eyes!

Permission Slip

We give permission for —————
to participate on the overnight 6th Grade Whale Watch and Plimoth Plantation Excursion Thursday and Friday, October 3 and 4.

Parent or Guardian

shows life in colonial America the Pilgrims. The trip has always been a great success.

The trip is Thursday and Friday, October 3 and 4. All students will stay at Ye Olde Plimoth Inne Thursday evening. Please sign the permission slip and send it back to school with your child no later than Friday, September 15.

We hope your child will be able to participate in this exciting experience.

This is going to make me famous someday.

It's the world's biggest ball of dried Marshmallow Fluff!! It's almost three pounds!

This is a lot harder to make than most people might think. You have to start with a little tiny ball the size of a booger and work your way up from there.

You have to wait for each layer to dry really well, or else you can't add the next coat of Fluff. Also, you can't work on a leather sofa, which I learned the hard way is super expensive to clean.

The ball is so big I had to make a little stand for it out of an empty toilet paper roll and a shoe box. I have to make sure to wrap it real well in plastic if I'm not working on it, otherwise ants can find it, which I also know from personal experience. My mom came into my room once and found a trazillion ants crawling all over it, and she screamed like she'd found someone murdered in my room or something.

The only thing left in my bag is this fuzz.
There's nothing left.
That's all there was.

Whale Watch Troubles

My alarm went off at five o'clock
As the sun rose in the skies.
"You ready?" my father asked,
Squirting water in my eyes. . . .

Yup, that's how my whale watching field trip started!!
It took three tries for Dad to get me up, so he finally
filled my Super Soaker and sprayed me in the face. Pop's
a real HOOT!!

My mom poured
me a bowl of ce-
real, which I mostly

dribbled down my shirt. She handed me a bag of snacks for the trip, gave me a kiss good-bye, and told me to behave myself. I don't think you can behave anyone except yourself, but I mumbled "Okay" just to make Mom happy.

I didn't say much on the drive to my school, 'cause even though my legs and arms were sort of moving around and my eyes were blinking, I wasn't awake, really, just pretending.

When we pulled into the school parking lot, there were already a lot of kids and parents there, lined up by the bus.

Dad gave me a thumbs-up and yelled "Good luck, Popeye!" as I ran to get in line. That's why everyone called me Popeye for the rest of the trip. Thanks a bunch, Dad!

I was the last person in line. The bus's motor was running, and I was standing where the exhaust came out. I was getting pretty woozy. Next thing I knew, I was on the ground, looking up at my teacher, Mrs. Claster, who wanted to know if I was all right. Seriously, flat on my back, my face gray from the fumes, and she asks me if I'm all right? *Um, no!*

But I told her I was anyway. I said the smoke just made me dizzy.

They called the school nurse, Mrs. Lavazzo, and the principal, Mr. Kretch.

I guess they were deciding whether I could go on the field trip.

There was NO WAY I was going to let them send me home.

First, Haley would never let me forget that I fainted before I even got on the bus.

Plus, my parents both work, and I didn't want to have our neighbor Mrs. Ulanski come stay with me AGAIN.

She watches Animal Planet all day, and if I see (or even hear) one more episode of *Kitten Kaboodles*, I might go bonkers!

So I got up and explained how President William Henry Harrison wouldn't let bus exhaust keep him from doing anything he wanted.

This didn't seem to help a whole lot. I heard Mrs. Lavazzo wonder if I was delirious.

I guess because I was the only kid in school who knew who President Harrison was, they let me go.

Kinda like extra credit.

Of course, by the time I got on the bus, there was only one seat left.

I'm CURSED!

> I climbed into the tour bus
> With 45 filled rows.
> There was only one seat left.
> Immediately I froze.
> I rode for six whole hours
> Sitting next to Ronny Bartz,
> A nice kid in many ways,
> But he burps a lot, and farts.

They showed a movie on teensy TV screens that dropped down from the top of the bus. They showed *Beverly Hills Chihuahua 5*. If you haven't seen it, you have two hours more of your life left than I do.

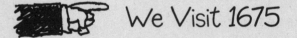 We Visit 1675

We stopped to visit the Olde Plimoth Plantation. It should be "Plymouth," but I guess the letters "y" and "u" weren't invented when the place was named. It's a little town that looks just like the one that the Pilgrims lived in, except they didn't have a gift shop or snack bar back then. But maybe way back then there was a little gift hut where you could buy a Plimoth Puritans T-shirt and a hot dog.

Everybody piled out of the bus. There were seventy-five kids, three teachers, and five parents called chaperones. I'm not sure, but I think *chaperone* is a word for someone who loves to ride in buses with a million screaming kids.

In Plimoth, they have actors who play the part of actual villagers. They walk around in hot, smelly wool clothes and talk in old-y English that's hard to understand.

Our guide was Master Timothy. He was real cheerful, and greeted us like he was our best bud. I couldn't tell exactly what he said, but when he asked if we had any questions "afore we start," everybody raised their hands and yelled out all at once.

"We gonna see you burn a WITCH?!"

"Hey, where'd everybody go to the bathroom back then?"

"How come you're sweatin' so bad?"

"How did Pilgrims charge their cell phones?"

"Was anyone here related to President Harrison?" (Guess who!)

"If I don't pee real soon, I'm having an accident right here in the town square."

Master Timothy started sweating something awful and suddenly remembered he had another tour he was supposed to meet. He left in a big hurry.

A lady named Mistress Hester took his place. She looked a whole lot less friendly. She had a scary-looking wooden rolling pin sticking out of her apron that I think had blood on it. She didn't say a lot. She walked super fast and said, "This be the bakery," "This be the butcher," and "This be the candlemaker." We were done with the whole two-hour tour in about twenty minutes!

When that was over, we went to a motel to spend the night! First time ever without ol' Mom and Dad. We stayed at Ye Olde Plimoth Inne. Instead of looking old-fashioned, like

the name, it just looked like any crummy old motel
to me.

Mrs. Claster told us to check in with our parent chaperone to get our room assignments. She told me I was
sharing a room with Ronald Bartz.

Now I was sure that there was no way this trip could
get much worse.

Just shows what I know.

We all ate dinner at the Pilgrims' Pizza Shack next door.
I had no idea the Pilgrims ate pizza and cheesesteaks,

but I guess that's why we take these educational field trips. I had three slices of pizza that had big pools of grease on them, and the only slices left by the time I could get to the trays had those smelly anchovy pieces on them. ECCCHHHH!!! But I was so hungry, I almost forgot to chew.

The motel had a small indoor pool, and most of us went in after dinner. The water was kind of weird. It was a little thicker than water usually is, like someone poured a few boxes of Jell-O in there. What made it worse, there were Band-Aids, hair ribbons, and strange specks floating around in it.

Maybe it was breathing in the bus smoke, or watching *Beverly Hills Chihuahua 5*, or sitting next to Ronald Bartz for three hours, or the greasy, nasty slices from the Pilgrims' Pizza Shack, or the pool water. I can't say for sure. But all of a sudden, I barfed right there in the shallow end.

Someone yelled, "Hey! Popeye just gooped in the pool!" There was a major riot as everyone tried to leave the pool at the same time.

The lifeguard looked at me like I had just pulled down my swim trunks and mooned his grandmother.

Everybody watched as he slowly walked over to get a long pool net, strolled back, fished out my three slices of half-chewed-up pizza that were floating in the water, went into the locker room, came back two minutes later with the empty net, and climbed back on his tall chair like nothing had ever happened. I couldn't believe it! I thought for sure they'd drain the pool.

"You okay?" Mrs. Claster asked me for the second time that day.

I nodded. "I just need to lie down for a little," I said. "I think it was the pizza."

"I'll walk him back to our room," someone said behind me.

Ronald Bartz.

We walked most of the way without saying anything.

We were climbing the stairs to our room when Ronald suddenly said, "I barf pretty often. I have a condition that gives me a lot of stomach problems."

When we got to our room, he said, "Hope you feel better," then turned around and headed back to the pool.

So now, besides feeling sick to my stomach, I felt

even worse for not talking to Ronald for three hours on the bus and writing that mean poem about him.

I never heard if anyone went back in the water with the floating Band-Aids, hair, belly-button fuzz, and I'm sure a few hunks of pizza.

 ## We Return to the Present. . . .

We got back on the bus early the next morning to get to the whale watch boat on time. I heard everyone talking about getting seasick, but I wasn't worried. I'd already thrown up, and figured I'd pretty much gotten that out of the way.

But just to be safe, I drank two glasses of ginger ale at the motel 'cause my mom says it's good for keeping your stomach calm. That turned out to be a HUGE mistake.

We got to the pier at nine o'clock and waited outside the office of Skipper Jack's Boat Adventures. Skipper Jack came out to greet us. I thought maybe he'd have a cool eye patch or tattoo or something like that.

No such luck. But he did have more hair growing out of his ears than I've ever seen before.

"Howdy, folks!" he shouted. "Welcome to my boat, the *Breakin' Wind*. We're headin' out to see some whales today, so I hope you're ready to shove off."

He gave us a lot of safety information, but I knew all this stuff already, because I've watched almost every episode of *Fish Tales*. It's a show where six boats go out into the dangerous Gulf of Mexico in a race to catch the most anchovies.

I know I wouldn't risk my life for the worst pizza topping ever, but I guess you can make a lot of money.

The sea seemed calm, but as soon as we left the little bay we were in, boy, did things change.

In five minutes we went from flat water to big waves that lifted the boat high in the air

and then dropped it so fast a GINORMOUS wave
crashed over the deck.

It seemed like everyone got seasick
at the exact same moment.

The waves tossed us up and down.
People hung over the rail
Moaning very loudly
And looking awfully pale.

Ronald and I were in the stern (the back of the boat, to rookie landlubbers who don't watch *Fish Tales* like me), and believe it or not, we were just fine. It's kind of funny that the kid who has stomach problems and the kid who threw up in the pool seemed to be the only ones not ready to toss their cookies.

Thank goodness, the waves finally got a little calmer.

"Hey, folks!" Skipper Jack announced over the boat's loudspeaker. "This is a real popular spot for humpback whales. We saw a pod of six out here yesterday. So keep a sharp lookout!"

Folks began to take out their binoculars and cameras, to be ready in case we got lucky.

Right about this time, my bladder was getting pretty full, and I could tell I was going to need a bathroom real soon. Immediately, actually.

I raced down three flights of skinny stairs

and then ran to the head (the bathroom, FYI. See how watching *Fish Tales* paid off?).

It was the teensiest bathroom ever. And it kind of smelled of the three hundred people who were in there before me, along with some dead fish and rotten seaweed.

I was minding my own business (or doing my own business) when I heard hoots, whistles, claps, and shouts of

"Thar she blows!"

I finished as fast as I could, zipped up, and washed my hands, but in that bathroom, it was sort of like wiping your feet in a coal mine!

I ran back up the stairs two steps at a time and reached the deck all out of breath.

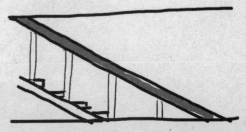

All around I heard shouts of "That was great!" and "Did you get that shot?" and "That was so COOL!"

Mrs. Bilnack, one of the parents, was dabbing her eyes with a Kleenex, saying, "That's something I'll tell my grandchildren about."

"What happened?!" I asked Ronald, who was standing at the railing.

"Oh, a humongous whale came up right by the boat, and he blew air out of his spout, and then his tail came WAY out of the water, and then he dove back down! You should have seen it!" He was trying to make me feel better, but instead it just made me feel worse.

I didn't give up. No way. I ran around the boat several times, hoping the whale would appear again. Of course there was nothing to see but plain old ocean.

The loudspeaker came on.

"Hey, folks, I'm glad you could see that, 'cause we're outta time, and they're predicting the seas are gonna pick up again. So we're hightailing it back to port."

It was cold and windy and started to rain, so everybody went inside the boat.

Except me. I was DISGUSTED! I didn't want to hear everybody yakking about how great it was to see a whale so close up that you could feel the spray from his tail. I missed everything, just because I have a very small bladder.

I stayed out in the wind and rain by myself, looking out the back of the boat.

Now, if you've found this journal somewhere and are reading it before you send it back to me, you're going to say that what I saw never happened.

But it did! FOR REAL!!

At first, it looked like a wave. But then I saw it was a fin. Then I saw the back of a dolphin cutting through the water. But something was kind of strange.

It was going straight through the waves, not coming up and going down, the way things happen on *Fish Tales*. Then the dolphin began rising out of the water!

I saw a whale lifting a dolphin out of the water! SHAZAAM! At first, I couldn't figure out if they were fighting or what. The dolphin slid into the water, and the whale disappeared.

I tried to call people to come see, but the wind blew my words back in my face. But I couldn't leave either. I'd missed enough for one day.

The same thing happened again a minute later.

The dolphin rode the back of the whale, rising higher and higher, till it fell off again.

No doubt about it, the whale was giving the dolphin rides. Maybe it's not the Nitro coaster at Six Flags, but for a dolphin it's still a lot of fun.

I watched one more time, then decided to spread the news. I ran down to the cabin and shouted, "You gotta see this! A whale is giving a dolphin a ride!!!"

Everyone just stared at me. "NO KIDDING!!"

Ronald shrugged and followed me, along with two pretty tough kids, Arnie Stims and Kincaid Johnson.

We stood at the rail for ten minutes. Nothing.

"I believe you," said Ronald.

"Yeah, me too, Popeye," snarled Arnie, giving my shoulder a sharp poke with his fist.

"You brought me out here for this?" asked Kincaid. "I was busy watching an octopus and a pelican playing poker!"

Kincaid and Arnie thought this was really funny and went back inside to tell everyone I was seeing things.

The boat returned to the dock. As soon as Skipper Jack put the gangplank down, everyone left right away for the bus.

I was just about the last one off. As I trotted past the captain, he whispered real loud, "I saw it, too." Then he pulled up the gangplank. He disappeared below to swab the decks, drop the anchor, clean the bathroom (yeah, right), and whatever other stuff skippers do at the end of a sail.

The ride home was really long, because we

drove the whole thing in one day. But it wasn't really that bad.

> I sat next to Ronald
> For the whole six hours,
> Talking about our heroes
> And their superpowers.
> I even thought of one for him:
> Gastro-Man, I think.
> No one flies behind him,
> Because he tends to stink.

We got back to the school at 9:30 at night, and I was beat.

"So, Popeye, how was your first time on the ocean?" Dad asked.

"Oh, it was great," I said, "I saw a dolphin surfing on a whale."

I guess Dad didn't know if I was joking, because he just gave me a weird look and didn't say a word all the way home.

I said the same thing when Mom asked me how the trip was, and guess what, it worked just as well with her!

"I'm really tired," I said. I dragged myself upstairs and fell into bed. No pajamas. No toothbrushing. No face washing. No shower.

I think my sneakers were still on.

Perhaps someday I'll try once more
(this is what I'm thinkin').
If I ever do whale-watch again,
You'll never see me drinkin'.

Halloween Troubles

No doubt about it, the MOST AWESOME day of the year—HALLOWEEN!

Oh, sure, Christmas is great for the gifts and being off from school.

Thanksgiving sure has the food thing, hands down. But I have to spend my whole day with the SUPER-BORING Hubbles from Columbus, and my mom's aunt Judith from New York City, who's just a pain! She gripes about everything, especially these weird things on her feet called bunions. I would give almost anything if she'd keep her shoes on when she visits. NO SUCH LUCK! Soon as she comes in, she sits on a chair, takes her shoes off, and rubs her twisted-up feet with toes that look like a small pile of elbow macaroni.

No, for real fun, there's nothing like H-Ween! When else can you dress up like a zombie or werewolf or super-hero and walk around your neighborhood and collect huge bags of candy?

There was only one choice of costume for me.

The RED SLOTH!

The main problem was going to be finding one. Oh, if you want to be Superman, Spider-Man, the Green Lantern, the Hulk, NO PROBLEM! There are stores that are only in business around Halloween, and there are RACKS and RACKS of those guys.

But the Red Sloth? Good luck, buddy! I only found one website on my dad's laptop for a company in Korea that sells them, and it says they're back-ordered. That's RIDICULOUS! I want to order the WHOLE COSTUME, not just the back.

I tried to get Mom to make a Red Sloth outfit for me, 'cause she's a whiz on the sewing machine if she wants to be. But she didn't. She said that her sewing machine needs a "new bobbin." Not sure what a bobbin is, but I think she's just making up excuses.

THANKS, MOM!

I had to think of something else.

Wednesday was trash day, and our neighbors the Rumpfs must have gotten a new refrigerator, 'cause there was a big cardboard box sitting out by the curb. I looked inside and there was a HUGE bag of those white peanuts people use to keep stuff from breaking.

I figured this could be the answer to my Red Sloth costume problem. I tipped the box over so I could reach the bag, but the end of the bag was open and a couple thousand peanuts blew all over the neighborhood!

Old Mr. Nussbaum saw this all happen, and he's sort of the neighborhood grump. He was yelling "HEY!

HEY, YOU!! CLEAN THIS UP!!!" so the whole block could hear it. I just grabbed what was left of the bag of peanuts and ran like crazy. I'm lucky Mr. Nussbaum uses a walker. Otherwise, I'm sure the mean old fart would've chased me.

I didn't tell anyone about my great idea for my Red Sloth costume. I wanted it to be a surprise. Besides, Dad was in a REAL bad mood when he came home.

"Some jerk dumped a bag of packing peanuts all over the neighborhood. I've been out there for twenty minutes picking them out of our bushes!"

"That stinks!" I agreed. Why start a big scene by telling him it was me?! I had lots to do and not much time

to do it, so I couldn't afford to be grounded or sent outside to pick up peanuts.

Ronny Bartz came over Halloween afternoon to help
me. He was going as Harry Potter, which is the easi-
est costume ever. I mean, (a) some round glasses, (b) a
wand, and (c) a lightning bolt on your head, and you're
done! Kind of lame, if you ask me. But I didn't say anything, especially 'cause I needed Ronny's help.

I found a HUGE hunk of red cloth in my mom's sewing closet. Pretty lucky, huh!

Harry Potter Costume Kit

Then I got the bag of packing peanuts, a pillow case
for my cape, a pile of art stuff, my mom's stapler, and
my dad's dental floss. I actually needed some real string,
but I couldn't find any.

FYI, Dad thinks dental floss is one of the greatest inventions ever. He used it to fix my kite and shorten some curtains, and when Haley was little he tied her hair up in a ponytail with dental floss when he couldn't find a real hair band. One Thanksgiving he even used it to tie up a turkey after it was stuffed. That came in handy for a couple people who could floss their teeth right there at the table!!!

We worked REAL HARD all afternoon, painting, stapling, cutting, and stuffing. When it was time, I wriggled inside, and Ronny tied my sleeves shut with about four feet of dental floss. Then we put the pillowcase around my neck with a safety pin.

I thought it looked pretty darn good. The main problem was I made a crinkly sound every time I moved or walked.

We went upstairs to show everybody. Haley was getting ready for the Halloween Dance at the high school. "Let me guess ... you're going as a tomato."

I told her that I was the Red Sloth. "Oh, right!" she laughed. "You're SO weird!"

When Mom saw me, she made a choking sort of sound and her eyes were watering. Probably swallowed wrong. But when she got her voice back she said I looked great!

It was getting dark already, so Ronny and I decided to skip dinner and get going.

It was hard walking in my costume, but that was OK, since the Red Sloth doesn't move that fast anyway. Worse than that was the crinkling sound, because it made it hard to talk with Ronny.

It was rough right from the start. Every time we came to a new house, the door would open and I'd hear,

"Oh, Harry Potter! And who on earth is THAT?" or "Oh, my!" or "Wow! That's . . . original."

Of course there were little kids everywhere, and they didn't like my Red Sloth costume, either. One girl dressed like a fairy princess started to cry, a boy in a Grover costume ran screaming to his dad, and a little pirate kid stabbed me with his sword.

Good thing it was rubber!

Nobody knows about the Red Sloth, so I had to explain it at every house we went to. It took an hour for us to do one side of one short block. All I had after ALL THAT TIME was a small pack of Twizzlers, a bag of M&M'S, some gum, five or six teeny chocolate bars, and a cherry Sour Straw.

I could hear Ronny was starting to have his stomach problems, and he hadn't even eaten any of his candy yet! We decided to head back toward his house.

There was one house I wanted to hit. Hope Ng's! She sits at my Losers' lunch table even though she's actually kind of popular. I think she's super pretty, and real soon I'm going to ask if she'd like to go to the first meeting of the Red Sloth Fan Club that I'm starting.

She'd appreciate my great costume for sure. Ronny and I walked up and rang her doorbell. I got all excited hearing footsteps behind the door. Hope opened it! "Henry? Is that you? Um, what are you . . . ?"

That was as far as she got, 'cause the WORST possible thing happened RIGHT THEN! I heard footsteps and laughing behind us.

"Hey! Look who it is! Harry Pooter and the Red Slob." It was Arnie Stims with devil's horns and a pitchfork.

I'm pretty sure it wasn't really even a costume, just his regular after-school clothes.

"Go away!" said Ronny, who now was in full fart mode.

"Whoa! That's nasty!" said Arnie, waving his hands in front of his face. "Guess I should go. But one last thing . . ."

He punched my backside. It didn't hurt, but I heard a loud rip. Packing peanuts started floating out of my costume's rear end.

I can't say what happened next was on purpose exactly, but I'm not gonna say I'm sorry, either.

I ran at Arnie and rammed him AS HARD AS

I *COULD*. He wasn't expecting me, dorky Henry Harrison Hubble, to do anything like that, so he wasn't ready for it. He flipped over the railing and landed in a holly bush by Hope's door!

Holly bushes have those prickly leaves, and he was doing some real loud yelling, including a whole bunch of words I get in trouble for saying at my house.

Ronny and I ran like crazy, 'cause Arnie wasn't going to be in that bush forever.

Actually about thirty seconds, I'd guess. Arnie pulled himself out and tore after us. I guess he twisted his ankle climbing out of the bush, otherwise Ronny and I would've been in DEEP sneakers!

There we were, Harry Potter WAY out in front, the Red Sloth in second place with packing peanuts streaming out his butt, and the devil limping along in last place, shaking his pitchfork and screaming.

Ronny peeled off as soon as he reached his street corner. "Good luck!" he yelled.

I just kept chugging, a heck of a lot faster than the REAL Red Sloth. Not fast enough, though!

Arnie was right behind me, so close he poked me twice with his pitchfork!!!

Maybe being SCARED TO DEATH helps you think up stuff, 'cause I had an AHA moment (that's what Dad yells every time he thinks of something all of a sudden). I reached into my trick-or-treat bag, ripped open both ends of the Sour Straw, turned around, and puffed as hard as I could. A cloud of sour dust sprayed all over Arnie's face.

That worked pretty GREAT!! He was coughing and rubbing his eyes and screaming more NASTY words, some I never even heard before!!

That gave me just enough time to round the corner to our driveway and head toward our front door.

I passed Haley, who was leaning against our lamp-post talking to the guy I thought was taking her to the dance.

"That's my bizarro baby brother," she said, trying real hard to be cool.

I just waved and smiled as I stumbled into the house. I didn't say a word about the packing peanut in Haley's hair that must've come from Mr. Nussbaum's refrigerator box. There were still thousands floating around the neighbors' houses.

I got in the door just in time to hear my dad yelling about his dental floss being empty.

My favorite day is Halloween—
Walking door to door,
Collecting pounds of candy,
Then heading out for more.

Be anything you want to be—
Hippie, pirate, Goth . . .
Or maybe a superhero,
Green Lantern or Red Sloth.

But if you get in trouble,
Snagged by demon claws,
Reach in your trick-or-treat bag,
For some cherry Sour Straws.

Lunchroom Troubles

Lunch is tough for me.

First, who do I sit with? In science we learned about the food chain. You know, what animal eats what other animal. In the school's food chain, I'm pretty much at the low end, where the plankton and brine shrimp are.

My lunch table is made up of pretty strange kids. Bad clothes, bad skin, bad breath, bad choice of clubs, and other weirdness. Besides me, the FOUNDER of the Losers' Table, here are the other current members:

Ronald Bartz (newest member, stomach gas problem, belongs to the Comix Club)

Amy "Mouse" Milman (really high voice, captain of the badminton team)

Phil Zupp (sousaphone player in the marching band, eyes blink all the time)

Ned Dorphy II (bad stutter, treasurer of the chess club)

Hope Ng (knows EVERY character in ALL seven Harry Potter books, president of the Harry Potter Fan Club, has a cat named Hufflepuff)

When I first met Hope I kinda wondered how you can you have a last name with no vowels in it. I tried saying "Ung" and "Nig," which had Hope laughing really hard. It turned out it's "Ing." It rhymes with "sing."

We all get along really well. The thing about lunch I enjoy most is sitting close to Hope, who I think is really pretty. She's very quiet, and I never know what to say, so we sure have silence in common.

I guess that's a start!

My real problem at lunch is Miss Vanderbeek. We got off on the wrong foot the very first day of school.

She overheard me telling Phillip Zupp that her mac 'n' cheese smelled like my aunt Edith's feet. I happen to know it's true, since Aunt Edith always takes her shoes off when she comes to our house at Thanksgiving.

Since then, Miss Vanderbeek gives me a nasty look every time I get in line.

Miss V's school lunches must be the worst in the

country, maybe the world. I once saw a TV show with this bald guy who goes around the world eating fried beetles, goats' brains, and bats' eyes. After every dish, he smiles and says some-thing like "It tastes like moldy fish, but it's not bad at all!"

Big deal! I'd like to see him come to the Orville Crumb Middle School and scarf down a big chunk of our City Chicken, or some of Miss Vanderbeek's famous Surprise Stew. Let's see who's still smiling then!

Things sort of came to a head during National School Lunch Week. Every kid in school was supposed to do a project about the importance of good nutrition. We had a Food Fest Friday, to show our work.

One class did a cooking contest like they have on Chow TV, except they all had to use healthy food, like bean sprouts and yogurt and stuff. Most of it looked pretty scary to me.

Arnie Stims, who likes to win at everything, brought in a Chicken-Style Pot Pie. It was called Chicken-Style because it was made with tofu instead of chicken. I hate tofu. If you haven't tried it, it's made with bean curd, which I think is just a misspelling. I tasted it one time, and I'm pretty sure *curd* is supposed to start with a *T*!!!

I stayed away from everything, until I got to Hope's dish. She brought in a big bowl of Vietnamese Shrimp and Lemongrass Noodle Salad.

I wanted to show her how interested I was in her family's culture, so I plopped a large helping on a plate and ate the whole thing.

I was actually surprised. Lemongrass tastes better than either lemons or grass. She smiled when I told her it was really delicious, so that was pretty nice.

Mrs. Claster said our class could do a "free" project for Food Fest, which meant we could more or less do anything we wanted.

Seeing as nobody in my house likes to cook, I decided I'd write a poem.

MENU FOR THE WEEK

Monday

Chocolate milk, warm and icky
Jell-O squares, hard but sticky
Hamburgers, thin and cold
Fruit cup with a little mold

Tuesday

Apple juice that tastes like water
Soup today: cream of otter
Our special stew, made from eels
Banana pie, including peels

Wednesday

Nacho chips with runny cheese
Vegetables with shriveled peas
Toads on toast with mushroom sauce
Brownies made from fresh peat moss

Thursday

Chopped-up squid with brownish goop
Cream of dandelion soup

Deep-fried seaweed fritters

Homemade pie with assorted critters

Friday

Lizard salad on whole wheat

Soup broth made from chicken feet

Turnip leaves by the bunch

I think today I'll bring my lunch!

Mrs. Claster said I could read my poem at the end of the Food Fest. Boy, was I excited! I could already hear the laughter and applause.

Best of all, I'd show Miss Vanderbeek who's who in the cafeteria. I could already imagine her hiding behind the steam table with her glasses all fogged up as soon as she saw me coming through the cafeteria door.

But funny thing: just before my turn my lips started to tingle really, really badly. I licked them, and they felt like they were twice their usual size! I poked them with my fingers, and I couldn't feel them at all! They were completely numb!

Just then, Mr. Kretch called my name, and I had to go up onstage to read my poem.

I held the microphone and began. . . .

> *"Minoo fa da wuk*
> *Chucklot muk, wum an ickuh,*
> *Jello scwuzz, wum ba stickuh*
> *Humbugga, din bu cole*
> *Fut caw wad a lidda mode ..."*

Just as I thought they would, all the kids started laughing really hard. But I think it had more to do with the fact that I could barely move my lips. Oh, yeah, and the fact that my huge lips made me look like a fish.

I guess I had an allergic reaction to the shrimp in Hope's noodle dish. At least, that's what Mrs. Lavazzo, the school nurse, told my mom when they spoke over the phone.

It took a long time for my dad to arrive, and I was getting

pretty bored and tired sitting in the nurse's office. I think I even dozed off a little.

Hope came into the nurse's office with my book bag. She said, "I'm so sorry about your face."

But guess what!? When the nurse walked away, Hope leaned over and kissed me on the cheek! Zowie!

I don't know. Maybe I was asleep and dreamed it.

I like to think I was awake.

Science Project Troubles

I guess I can write about this now, two months after it happened. Nobody mentions it much anymore. Yahoo!

This year in science we're studying plants and animals. My teacher is Mr. Moster. He's almost as interesting as the back of a cereal box.

When he's teaching, he sits in his chair and leans way, way back with his hands behind his head, so everybody can see his armpit stains.

One time Mr. Moster leaned so far back, his chair tipped over. All we could see were his shoes sticking above his desk. So far that's the only interesting thing that's happened in his class.

Mr. Moster told us the first day of the semester that we had to do a project on mammals. We could pick any mammal we wanted—mice, lions, camels, monkeys, humans, anything with fur that feeds its babies with milk.

Ned Dorphy II has to drink soy milk, which is made from a vegetable. I wonder if he's a mammal. I have to remember to ask him.

I can't say what happened exactly. I thought my mammal project was due on a Friday, but it turns out it was the Monday before. I guess Mr. M. reminded us during class, but sometimes I'm not paying super-close attention. Maybe I was drawing the Red Sloth in my notebook, or thinking about Hope Ng in the next row, or wondering how I was going to honor President Harrison's birthday on February 9.

Whenever he made the announcement, I somehow missed it.

I knew I was in trouble right away on Monday morning, when Ronald called to offer me a ride to school. His dad was driving him because he had a large model of a hippopotamus to take in, and he thought maybe I had something like that, too.

I asked why he was taking it in today, and he said, "Duh-uh! Because it's due today, dummy!"

I didn't even say bye. I just hung up and ran to my room.

It was a good thing I had already made some notes for my project, which was on squirrels.

Why squirrels? They're amazing! I once saw one fall from the top of a really tall tree. I was sure I'd see a squirrel-guts explosion when he hit the ground, like a water balloon, only red and lots chunkier. But he just landed in the grass and ran away!

My dad hates squirrels. He calls them country rats. He's always trying to chase them out of our yard,

but they don't seem to stay away for more than five minutes.

He bought a "squirrel-proof" bird feeder. It has a bar that birds can sit on to eat seeds but that snaps the door shut if a squirrel climbs on it. Dad laughs real hard every time he sees a squirrel creep up the pole to the feeder and then fall to the ground when the bar clunks down.

One time he went out to fill the feeder with bird-seed and lifted the lid. A squirrel shot out of there like a ROCKET. It had somehow gotten inside and was stuffing its face with seeds. Dad came in the house screaming about how the squirrel almost made him wet his pants.

Now, THAT'S an animal I want to do a project about!

I stuffed all my notes into my book bag and ran to catch my bus. I already figured Mr. Moster was going to give me a D- for the worst project ever.

I was almost at my bus stop when a squirrel ran by me, and I had another AHA moment. I realized I could have the best science project in the history of the Orville Crumb Middle School.

I took all my junk out of my book bag and dug out my ball of dried Marshmallow Fluff. I aimed real carefully and rolled it over to the squirrel. I knew this might ruin my chances to be a celebrity for having the world's biggest fluff ball, but, hey, this was an emergency!

Big-time.

The squirrel sniffed the ball, grabbed it with its teeth, and dragged it behind a tree. I took everything out of my book bag and slowly crept around the tree.

I saw this same trick once on a show where they dropped this English guy into some horrible swamp with no tools or gun or anything and he had to trap lizards and birds with his bare hands. Of course, he didn't have a ball of Marshmallow Fluff, or a Walmart book bag like mine, but otherwise, it was pretty similar.

I swung the bag as fast as I could. The squirrel would've gotten away, except the Marshmallow Fluff ball stuck to his fur, which slowed him down a lot. Oh, snap! I got him! I zipped up my bag, and the squirrel wasn't too happy, especially after I jammed everything back in there.

I picked up the rest of my stuff and ran to the bus, which was sitting there waiting for me with its blinkers going. Mr. Nitz, our bus driver, gave me a dirty look when I climbed up the steps.

I sat next to

some kid named Paul and just minded my own business.
Tried to, anyway.

Paul got kind of excited when he heard squeaks and
chirps coming from my book bag. And when the bag
rolled onto its side and started moving, he hollered so
loud everyone looked at us.

I gave the bag a little poke and explained we had gotten it on sale at Walmart, so weird things happened a lot.

The squirrel calmed down the rest of the way to school, thank goodness. I ran to my locker and shoved my book bag in really fast. I don't have science until ten-thirty, and I didn't want to be walking around with the squirrel all that time.

I couldn't wait for ten-thirty to come. I was sure Mr. Moster was going to be thrilled with my sharp thinking, using a real animal in my mammal project.

I got my bag after second period was over. The squirrel must have been tired from all the excitement, because he wasn't moving. Not even a twitch.

I had to wait for a couple kids to give their presentations. Ronald Bartz showed his three-foot-high model of a hippopotamus. It had the legs of a doll sticking out of its mouth, because hippos kill more humans in Africa than any other wild animal, including lions, tigers, or snakes. So that was pretty cool.

Finally! It was my turn! I went up to the front of the class with my book bag. I wanted to show the squirrel at just the right moment.

"My project is about the common squirrel," I began. "People don't notice them much, but they're actually very smart and strong animals that can do amazing things."

I unzipped my bag and tried to gently bring the squirrel out to show everybody. The squirrel had other ideas, though, 'cause he shot out of my bag and landed smack on the back of Mr. Moster's head.

Mr. M. screamed and staggered around, knocking everything over. The whole class was yelling and running around the room looking for places to hide.

All of a sudden the squirrel jumped off Mr. M. and ran out the door. There were classes in the hall lined up for early lunch, and I could hear all this screaming and shouting and saw kids running every which way.

I chased the squirrel into the art room. I heard lots more screaming as he ran over everyone's wet paintings, getting paw prints all over.

Mr. Hintzil, the janitor, showed up with all kinds of brooms and blankets. He cornered the squirrel under a desk, and I really thought he had it. But somehow it escaped.

I ran back to my locker to get what was left of the Marshmallow Fluff ball. Maybe we could catch the squirrel with that. You know, even though I knew I was in big trouble, I felt sorry for the squirrel. One minute he's eating a tasty ball of Marshmallow Fluff, and the next he's being chased through a school with brooms and hundreds of screaming kids.

I got back to the art room just in time to see the squirrel jump through a broken window in the back of the room, just like that.

A minute later the intercom went on with a ding.

"This is Principal Kretch. Students, faculty, don't be alarmed. We can all breathe easy now. Our friend the squirrel is out of the building. Please go to your homerooms so we can see if everybody's okay, and then we'll resume our normal day."

The speakers turned off.
Then they dinged again.
"Would Henry Hubble please come to the office immediately."

Perhaps you're wondering
How my project ended.
I got a big fat F,
And I got suspended.

Discipline Slip Troubles

Actually, I wasn't REALLY suspended, where they call your parents and you have to go home right away. But I had to spend the day in in-school suspension in the library.

Mrs. Neffler, the librarian, told me to sit and read. Just in case Hope walked by, I picked out *Harry Potter and the Order of the Phoenix*. She LOVES everything about Harry Potter and probably has posters of that actor Daniel Radcliffe all over her room. Lucky dude!

I guess the *Order of the Phoenix* is the fourth or fifth book, but I've never read any of them, so I'm not sure.

I opened it to page 491, like I was in the middle of the story, which would REALLY score points with Hope.

The whole day Mrs. Neffler just kept looking at me and shaking her head and making that *tsk tsk tsk* sound grown-ups always make when they think you screwed up.

That part wasn't so bad. I was more spooked by the discipline slip Mr. Moster gave me, telling my parents how I'd brought a live squirrel to school. It said I'd "caused panic among the students and put the school staff at risk trying to capture a wild animal that might have bitten them and was possibly carrying rodent-borne disease."

That last part about the squirrel having germs was TOTALLY bogus. Anyone could see he was completely healthy. You can't jump 15 feet from a desk to the back of a guy's neck in one second if you're sick.

Course, there was a blank line at the bottom of the note where my parents had to sign.

That was the tricky part, picking Mom or Dad to sign the note.

Mom has this thing about animals. She says "awwwwwwwww" every time she sees a rabbit, a deer, a raccoon, even a possum, and I think possums are the goofiest-looking animals ever. So I was pretty sure she wouldn't like me stuffing a squirrel in my book bag and dragging him off to school.

Plus, Mom's much stricter than Dad. If I do something bad, Dad will sometimes just wink and say, "Don't do that again, Henry." This makes Mom go ballistic, and usually causes a HUGE argument. She always complains about having to be the family disciplinarian and how she

and Dad are supposed to be "on the same page." I sure wish I knew where that page is so I could read it ahead of time.

But Dad's not a good choice, either. He's a hypochondriac, which is someone who thinks he's sick or going to be sick real soon. So he's always spraying counters and handles with all kinds of cleaners to kill germs. When he reads that line about "rodent-borne disease," he'll go nuts. I bet he knows at least seven diseases you can catch from squirrels.

I've heard that sometimes people sleepwalk to the refrigerator in the middle of the night and eat huge snacks without remembering anything about it the next day. I thought about staying up late at night to see if either Mom or Dad gets up for a midnight bag of Oreos. It would be a great time to get one of them to sign

the slip! I needed the signature RIGHT AWAY, so I had to try THAT NIGHT. . . .

No surprise!! It didn't work.

I tiptoed down to the kitchen after Mom and Dad thought I was asleep and hid in the pantry. I was hoping to catch one of them in the middle of the night stumbling to the refrigerator like a zombie, get my slip signed, and go back to bed.

Instead, my dad found me asleep in the pantry around midnight. He asked me what I was doing in there, but fortunately, I didn't give anything away, or drop the note. Close call!

The answer to my problem hit me while I was sleeping, and I woke up all of a sudden at six o'clock. The answer was so simple! I'd just sign the slip for them. It wasn't like I was going to bring another squirrel to school. No way. I learned my lesson.

So really, what was having one of my folks sign a piece of paper going to help? Nothing!

Plus, I'm a good artist, so I figured I could copy a signature, no sweat!

I got up very quietly and took the slip into my parents' office. I decided to sign for Mom, because her first name is Dawn and my dad's is Hamilton. So that's four letters instead of eight, which is half as many.

The hard part was finding Mom's signature somewhere so I could copy it. It took me fifteen minutes of looking through a bunch of drawers and folders, but I finally found a check she'd written to Bloomingdale's. It was for $375!! I got goose bumps thinking of all the Red Sloth comics I could buy with that.

My folks' alarm goes off at six-thirty, so I had maybe fifteen minutes left before they were up. I put the check underneath the slip and lined up her name so it showed through, right on the line. I started to write *D-A-W*. . .

"Hey! Whatcha doin'?" It was Haley. I kind of screamed. I forgot she gets up a half hour before Mom and Dad to catch her bus!

I told her I was sending someone a President Harrison's

Day card, then ran to my room with the discipline slip scrunched in my hand.

When I got back to my room, I looked at the slip. The *W* went right off the page.

Aghhhhhhhh!

When I heard Haley in the hall bathroom blowing her hair dry, I ran back to the office and found a bottle of that white-out goop people use to cover up mistakes. It was so old I had to use pliers to get the top off. The stuff looked more like toothpaste, only with big lumps in it.

I painted over the ink as best as I could and smoothed it out with my finger. I heard Mom walking around, so

I quickly signed the rest of her name without lining up the check, just trying to get done as fast as I could.

This is the slip—I really thought it would do the trick if Mr. Moster didn't look too closely.

Dear Mr. and Mrs. Hubble,

I'm afraid that there was a problem in class today that involved Henry. He brought a live squirrel into the school building as part of a "visual aid" for a science project on mammals in Mr. Moster's class.

The squirrel escaped into the building, which caused a tremendous disruption and panic among students and staff. We were concerned that the frightened animal might have bitten someone, exposing them to possible rodent-borne disease.

Please sign this slip, so that we know you've spoken to Henry about this serious school infraction.

—Linus Kretch (Principal)

Parent or Guardian _Dawn D. Hubble_

I had a couple more close calls before I left for school. Dad wanted to know what the white stuff on my hand was. That wasn't too hard, because everyone knows cartoonists use paint all the time. But I could hear Mom screaming, "Who messed up my desk?!" and "Why is this Bloomingdale's check sitting out here?!?"

I stuffed a granola bar into my mouth.

"Gotta go!" I yelled, spraying oats and raisins every-where. I grabbed my book bag—which was pretty torn up and still had some squirrel droppings rolling around the bottom—jammed my note between my lips, and ran out the door.

I was super nervous all the way to school. I kept try-ing out different greetings for Mr. Moster.

"Hey, Mr. Moster, here's that signed note you needed. I'll sure never do that again! Ha ha!"

"Mr. Moster, my bad bringing the squirrel to school. Good thing no one can even see those scratches under your collar!"

But when I got to science class, I decided to keep it simple. I just handed the slip to Mr. Moster, gave him a sad sort of look, and sat down at my desk.

At first I thought Mr. M. was having a fit or something! His eyes were squeezed shut and his body was shaking some-thing fierce, but he wasn't making a sound. Tears were running down his cheeks. He kind of staggered out of the room holding my slip.

That was when I heard screams of laughter out in the hall. First from Mr. Moster. But then I heard Ms. Costallano (the Spanish teacher) next door, then Mr. Posner (American History) across the hall, and Mrs. Claster. Then I lost track. It was like a comedian was doing a show in the second-floor corridor of Orville Crumb Middle School.

Mr. Moster came back in the room, kind of puffing "Hoo! ... Hoo! ... Hoo!" and wiping his eyes with a Kleenex.

"Wow, Henry, that was great. Thanks! You made my day! That's probably the worst job of forging a parent's signature in the history of the school." He sat down at his desk and scribbled a note.

"But you still have to take this to Mr. Kretch's office."

I'm sitting once more
In the principal's office.
Not feeling too well—
In fact, pretty nauseous.
My advice to you,

If you get such a slip,
Is to hold your pen
With a very firm grip.

Attic Troubles

Mom and Dad must've worked out that being "on the same page" thing, because they came into my bedroom together and told me I was grounded for two whole weeks. One week for taking the squirrel to school, and one week for faking Mom's signature on the discipline slip.

Give me a break!

So I had 14 days with LOTS of time on my hands.

At least I was allowed to watch "educational programs" some of the time.

The American History Channel was doing a special two-week series, *President Who?* Every night they covered the lives of some US presidents no one gives a hoot about.

I had to sit through five BOOORRRRING nights before they got to my guy, William Henry Harrison. But he only got fifteen minutes, and they didn't even mention Jupiter! That's insane!!! I had to let them know what a lousy job they did.

I have to share an old laptop with Haley. It has a cracked screen and makes this weird chirping sound, and I think I've seen smoke coming out of it once or twice.

But it sort of works, except for the G, which sticks a few seconds, so there are words like *singgggg* and *gggggglow* that you have to go back and fix.

I actually got the laptop away from Haley long enough to send my email to the American History Channel, to gripe about their measly fifteen minutes on W.H.H.

I printed it out so I'd have a record.

Dear American History Channel,

What's the matter with you guys?! I waited for a whole week to hear about my favorite president, William Henry Harrison, who I'm kind of named after! And you gave him a cheesy fifteen minutes!

Okay, I didn't know he was a hero in the War of 1812, so that was cool. But you didn't even mention his dog, Jupiter, who took dumps in my great-great-great-great-grandmother's yard when he lived in Columbus, Ohio.

BTW, we have some ACTUAL JUPITER POOP from all that time ago in a bottle in our attic. Would anybody at your company know how much that's worth? If someone there can help me figure that out, it would be really great.

So let's do a better job next time!

Henry Harrison Hubble

I really wasn't expecting to hear back from them. But two days later, I actually got this email!!!

Dear Henry,

Thanks for taking the time to contact us concerning our series *President Who?* It's wonderful to hear from a young person who takes such interest in our nation's history.

We're sorry you were disappointed in the airtime we were able to give to President Harrison. But as he only served thirty-two days in office before his untimely death, there just wasn't a lot of material to work with. You can be sure that had he lived out his full term, he certainly would have been among our finest leaders.

Regarding the jar of dog "poop" you described, unfortunately no one here can offer you much help. Even with today's amazing scientific tools, it would be impossible to prove which dog that actually came from and who its rightful owner might have been at that time. Even if all of that could be proven, we don't think that dog excrement, even of this historical importance, has a significant dollar value.

However, as with any family heirloom, Jupiter's gift to your relative should be kept with pride and cherished as a true piece of American history.

We value your feedback!

The staff at AHC

Okay, it was nice to hear back from those guys, but I was totally bummed. I'd figured that Jupiter's jar would bring in enough money for me to buy an Xbox, a new bike, or at least some Red Sloth comic books.

But I began to wonder about Ida Rosabelle Hubble with her jar of Jupe poop. I mean, who does that? I decided I'd explore our attic to see what other stuff I.R.H. might have left for us.

It was Saturday, so I had nothing else to do, what with being grounded and all. Haley was "babysitting" me. She gets paid for that!! WHAT A JOKE!!

I grabbed a flashlight from the kitchen and went straight to the upstairs linen closet. It has the trapdoor we use to get into the attic. I was a little nervous. It's pretty dark up there, and in movies that's always where all the gory stuff happens! My hands were shaking, so it wasn't so easy to yank the cord hard enough to pull the folding steps down.

When I climbed up, I shot the flashlight around, just like you see on all the cop shows. There were old boxes everywhere, plus stuffed animals and baby junk left over from Haley and me.

There was also a bunch of water jugs, canned soup, first-aid stuff, and ten cans of Lysol antigerm spray Dad had dragged up there just in case there was a tornado,

an earthquake, a zombie invasion, or some other big disaster.

If the zombies do come, we'll be out of luck, because the water jugs were empty, and the soup cans had rust all over them. I'm sure no expert, but I don't think it helps to spray zombies with Lysol.

Way, way, WAY in the back I found an old black trunk with stickers from different cities all over it. Oh, yeah!

I opened it and shined the flashlight in there. There were some old blankets and clothes, a winter coat, gloves, a hairbrush, knitting needles, and a stuffed rabbit with one eye missing. I threw all that stuff on the attic floor.

At the very bottom was a big leather bag. I figured this must be it. It wasn't so easy to open, the leather was so old and stiff.

I found the bottle right away. It had weird writing on it.

Jupiter Harrison
412 Bay Street
Columbus, Ohio
August 7, 1826

I gave it a good shake and heard something rattling inside. At first I thought about opening it. But I gave up on that. I didn't care if it was historical. No way I was going to smell two-hundred-year-old dog poop!!

I looked deeper in the bag. There was an old envelope. It read *To Magistrate J. Warren*. I opened it REALLY slowly, because little bits fell off every time I moved it. There was a note inside! How cool!

When I unfolded the paper, I saw it was in the same handwriting. That was hard enough to read—it took me FOREVER to figure out all the fancy-pants words no one uses anymore, but I hung in there!

Here's the letter. If you're somewhere reading this journal, be extra careful turning this page, on account of the paper crumbles real easily.

Ida Rosabelle Hubble
412 Bay Street
Columbus, Ohio

To His Honorable Magistrate Josiah Warren,

I have attempted to resolve this issue through every means at my disposal, but at long last, I must make this official complaint.

On numerous occasions, I have appealed to my neighbor Senator W. H. Harrison's sense of common decency in restraining his dog, Jupiter, from performing various bodily functions within the confines of my property.

Senator or not, he has proven himself most unsympathetic to my petitions.

The specimen I present to you herewith should be proof enough of the continuing threats to my health and my footwear. I hope you will bring the full weight of your esteemed office to enforcing the law regarding this matter.

Most respectfully yours,
Ida Rosabelle Hubble

This was so GREAT!! An actual letter from all that time ago! Plus, this was TOTAL proof that ol' Ida lived next door to Will H. H., even if he was a COMPLETE jerk as a dog owner.

And best of all, it proved she wasn't totally nuts, keeping dog poop in a jar! I'd been a little worried about that, wondering if there could be some built-in insanity in our family.

I got so excited, I started bouncing all over the place.

For anyone reading my journal, attics don't always have floors everywhere.

I know this because I jumped one time too many and my feet sank into that pink cotton-candy stuff they put up in the attic to keep your house warm.

Then there was crunching and cracking, and the next thing I knew, I fell out of the attic. I landed in our bathtub, looking at Haley wrapped in a towel, painting her toenails.

Of course, Haley screamed.

A bottle of poop, a mysterious letter.
Now I know Ida Hubble much better.
I thought she might be some weird dog
*   fanatic,*

But that's not what I found in the trunk in
    my attic!
I'm glad I went up there, that's my true
    feeling,
Even now, while I help my dad patch the
    ceiling.

Valentine's Day Troubles

None of this would have happened if I had a YourFace page like everyone else. Mom and Dad say I'm not "mature" enough to have one. OK, I admit I dive-bombed our neighbor's smelly cat, Jezebel, with my remote-control XR7 DynoBlaster helicopter last week.

But otherwise I'm TOTALLY mature.

I wouldn't put it past Mom or Dad to be checking my computer history to spy on me, just in case I tried to start a YourFace page. And anyway, I practically have to wrestle Haley to get to use the laptop, so it doesn't make much difference.

Things are getting hairy at lunch, 'cause Hope invited Miles Bumgarten to our Losers' Table. I guess he must like Hope, 'cause he ACTUALLY SAT DOWN WITH US!! Miles is like the smartest kid in our grade. He can point to Peru on a map without even thinking about it, and he can tell you who the president of India is—WITHOUT LOOKING ONLINE!

Oh, yeah, and he's editor of the school paper, the *Crumb Hollow Bugle*, AND captain of the school soccer team.

How is it possible for one kid to have all the good stuff!? Whoever hands out personal qualities needs to do a BETTER JOB!!!

So I have good reasons to be worried about Hope. I figured Valentine's Day would be a good time to make my move. If I had a YourFace page, it would be so easy to send her a little message about how much I like sitting behind her in science class and end with one of those heart thingies you can make with a keyboard: <3 . But I had no way to send her a cool V-Day message letting her know I think she's really special.

No one in middle school uses those paper cards any-more, the ones that say dumb stuff like *Be Mine* and

Yours Forever. The last time we gave those out was in fourth grade, and by accident I dropped a valentine into Paul Galupnic's bag instead of Paula Gallup's. That's a pretty easy mistake to make, but Paul made a HUGE deal about it right in the middle of class. Everyone had a good laugh. My bad.

I was pretty stuck about what to do. I finally decided to go with my specialties—cartoons and poetry! Here's what I came up with:

> *I like to dream about Hope Ng*
> *More than almost anythNg.*
> *There's lots of reasons, large and small,*
> *Sometimes for no reason at all.*
> *It makes me feel just like a kNg*
> *Sitting at lunch with you, Hope Ng.*

That sounded about right. I didn't want it too mushy. I signed it on the back. I folded it up REALLY

YOU'RE SUPER!

carefully and put it inside a red envelope with a heart on the front.

I wanted her to get it on Valentine's Day, so I went by her locker (#114) just before I left school the day before and slipped it inside.

I was pretty excited that night, wondering what Hope was going to think when she saw the coolest valentine ever, made just for her. I didn't sleep much because my mind was going a hundred miles an hour.

As soon as I got to school the next day, I waited by the stairway close to Hope's locker so I could pretend to be just strolling by when she found my card in her locker.

When she opened her locker, she looked down, and I thought, OH, BOY! HERE WE GO!!! But she just bent down and picked up her field hockey stick, got her books, and left!!!

WHAT HAPPENED????

While I was scratching my head over that, the kid with the locker next to hers says, "What's this?" It was Paul Galupnic!!! He had my red envelope in his hand. I had put it in the wrong locker!!!!

GAAAAAHHHHHHHHH!!

I raced over and grabbed the card right out of his hand!

"HEY! Whattaryadoing, weirdo?!"

"Oops! Sorry!" I ran down the hall, bumping into lousy old Miss Vanderbeek and about four other kids on the way.

That was CLOSE!!

But now I had the problem of getting my gift to Hope on Valentine's Day. Of course, I'd see her at lunch, but then everyone would be there to see me give her a red envelope with a heart on it. No, I had to try something else.

I'd seen this video clip on TV once, taken by this guy who was the pilot of a small plane. He proposed to his girlfriend by pretending the plane they were flying in was going to crash. He had her read the emergency landing instructions out loud, which ended "Put the ring on the fourth finger of your left hand" and "Say you'll marry me!" What a fun way to get engaged!!

I'm not asking Hope to

marry me right now, but I'd like to surprise her in a romantic way like that.

Hope is in Mr. Moster's science class with me. We were on the second day of dissecting a frog. So far we had only gotten our frogs stuck onto the wax with big pins.

Everybody had their own pan, so I found the one with Hope's name on it and carefully slipped my card right under her frog. Sure, it would get a little of that smelly chemical stuff on it, but I figured that wasn't a big deal, really.

This surprise frog thing wasn't as great as making a girl think she was going to die in a plane crash, but it was still pretty good.

The bell rang, and everybody sat at their desks. I was all goose-bumpy with excitement! Mr. Moster came in.

"OK, everyone. Let's pick up again where we ended last time with our frog dissections. Everybody go back to the benches with your frogs and we'll get started."

I was just about jumping out of my own skin, waiting to see Hope find my envelope under her frog.

Mr. Moster came back to give us instructions about what to do next.

"OK, everybody, let's all gather around Hope's spot so I can show you how to proceed."

No. No. NO. NO. NO! NO! NO! NO!!

I tried to think of possible ways to avoid the WORST FAIL EVER!!!! I could pull the fire alarm. I'd be suspended (again!), but that couldn't be worse than what was about to happen.

"What's THIS?"

Too late.

Mr. Moster pulled the note out from under the frog,

who was in A LOT better shape than I was right then. He looked around from kid to kid, and I guess he saw that my face was all red and sweaty.

"Uh, Mr. Hubble, is this yours?"

"Oh, I was wondering where that was. Heh heh."

"Ms. Ng, you can pick up your mail at the end of class."

The whole class laughed and giggled. My head felt so hot, I thought my hair might catch fire. Hope just looked down without saying a word.

I don't remember much about the rest of class, really. I don't even remember anything about the frog. Or which creep put it in my book bag.

At lunch, I sat at the other end of the table from Hope. I wasn't hungry AT ALL.

I was pretty sure life couldn't get ANY WORSE. I picked up my lunch and went to the trash bin to toss it. Hope was right behind me. Oh, brother.

"Henry, you dropped something." She walked right by me. A piece of paper fell by her feet.

I picked it up. . . .

That was sweet.

Dance Troubles

The OCMS Spring Dance was just a week after the Great Valentine's Day Frog Episode. I usually wouldn't go to that on a BET. Going to a dance is just ASKING for trouble, and I've proven that trouble finds me all on its own.

But now I had HOPE'S NOTE—I looked at it about ten times a day—I decided I had to go, just in case she was there.

I knew there were risks! Arnie Stimms might be there. Miss Vanderbeek might be one of the chaperones. And of course, I CAN'T DANCE. So there were HUGE opportunities for disaster.

I watched an episode of *Celebrity Dance-a-Thon* to

see if I could pick up some tips, but it was NO HELP AT ALL!! OK, the women dancers were all super beautiful, but otherwise it was a TOTAL waste of time. I'm pretty sure nobody under 60 does the cha-cha anymore!

I figured I'd just go and copy what everyone else was doing, if I got a chance to dance with Hope.

Mom said I should wear a shirt and a tie. YEAH, RIGHT!!!! Was she TRYING to get me KILLED???? Maybe I should take a little briefcase, too, and a SpongeBob beanie.

I told her I knew what to wear, even though I really didn't. I just decided to put on some jeans and a sweatshirt. Nothing scary there. But I did go into my dad's bathroom cabinet and found a jar of Tomahawk styling gel for my hair.

I thought that sounded pretty cool. My hair usually looks like the bristles on a really old broom, with spiky things sticking out every which way. So I pulled out a nice glob of gel and carefully put it on my hair, right in front.

"Hey, bud, whatcha doin'?"

Dad darn near made me wet my pants when he came in like that. I was so freaked I got some gel in my left eye, which stung like CRAZY and made it pretty hard to blink.

"Oh, nothin', just getting ready for the dance!"

I went back to my room to check out my poor eyeball more carefully. It was all watery and red, with tears running down one side of my face. No matter how many times I washed it, my eyelids stuck together, so that my right eye blinked but my left only opened halfway.

PERFECT!!!! I seriously considered looking for the eye patch I still had from a pirate costume I wore one Halloween, but could already hear the shouts of "Hey, Bluebeard!" and "Ahoy, matey!"

No, I'd have to hope that by the time I got to the dance, my eye would be back to normal.

I heard a honk. It was Mr. Bartz, who was driving Ronny, Ned Dorphy, and me. I grabbed a baseball cap, shoved it as far as I could over my face, and yelled, "Gotta go!"

I heard Mom yell "Have" but the door slammed shut before the "fun!"

I got in the car with a quick "Hey!" and sat next to Ned.

"Whoa! What happened to your eye?"

"Um, oh, that! It's nothing. Got some dirt in it some- how. It's getting better already."

"If you say so. Looks pretty gross!"

When we got to the school we piled out of the car and headed for the gym, where the dance was. It was actually pretty dark in there. Good thing, too!

Mr. Kretch was right at the door, greeting the students.

"Mr. Hubble, what happened to your eye?"

I blurted out the first thing I could think of. "Rugby practice!" I don't even really know what rugby is, but I got past Mr. Kretch before he could ask what the heck I was talking about.

We went to the snack table to pretend to eat while we checked everything out. The girls were all in a bunch in the middle of the gym, laughing and talking. Hope was there! Hooo boy!

I waited for just the right moment to walk up to her. And waited. And waited. And waited.

FINALLY, the girls' group broke up, and they started playing some song "Hugz&Kisses." This was it. . . .

Until Miles Bumgarten walked up to Hope, whispered in her ear, and took her to the center of the dance floor!!!!!!!!!!!!!!!!!!!!!!!!!!!!!!!!!!!!!!

Oh, did I mention that Miles Bumgarten is a DANCE WIZARD??!! The three other couples out there just gave up. Everyone just stood around and clapped while Miles made all these robot moves, flips, flops, dives, and twirls around Hope, who was laughing like crazy.

GAAAAAAAAGHGHGHGHGHGHGHGH!

I couldn't watch. Even with my GOOD eye.

I went to the snack table and held on like a guy who was about to go overboard on *Fish Tales*!!

Finally the song stopped. There was more clapping and hoots of "Wow!" and "Oh, boy!"

Miles must've headed for the bathroom to wash the sweat off or something. Hope was coming toward me, giggling and out of breath. I thought I might as well try to say something. I figured she probably needed a drink, so I grabbed a cup of fruit punch from the table.

"Hey, you were GREAT out there!"

"Ooh! What happened to your eye?!"

I don't know why, but I decided to try the truth.

"I used hair gel on my eyelashes. Does it look good?"

Hope laughed really hard at that.

Okay, that was COOL!

Snap! Just when I was starting to have fun, Miles came back. I finally remembered the cup of punch in my hand. I tried to give it to Hope before he got to us. "This is for you."

I guess it was 'cause of my left eye not working very well, and me being in a rush to hand the cup to Hope right away. Can't say for sure. But I tripped, and the drink spilled all over Miles.

He looked down at his sweater for a REALLY long time. Then he looked at ME. He grabbed my shirt.

"This sweater was the last thing my granddad ever gave me, dork! You're a DEAD MAN!!"

He stomped off, but I didn't feel any better AT ALL.

First of all, I felt really bad about splashing punch on Miles's sweater. I sure know how important things from your dead relatives can be. I'd be TOTALLY CRUSHED if someone threw out Ida Hubble's Jupiter jar.

I was pretty worried,

too, because Miles is so good at everything he does. He's probably great at killing people, too.

But I didn't see him in the gym anywhere, so I figured I'd have to wait until tomorrow. Hopefully, I'd still be ALIVE!

The only good thing was now I could finally try a dance with Hope without Miles hogging the floor. I just needed the right song to make my move.

"Kiss'N'Tell" (by Shanay-V.)?

Too risky.

"Forever Alwayz" (by Gassteroid)?

WAY, *WAY* too serious.

"We'll Never Make It" (by HeeZo Sick)?

Duh, no!

I was running out of time, fast. It was 9:50 and the dance was over at 10:00!! They played this weird song "Monkey Pants." Ugh. Well, it was now or never.

My legs were pretty shaky, but I went up to Hope and asked if she wanted to dance.

She gave a small shrug, the kind you'd give if you were starving to death in a desert and someone offered you a broccoli-flavored gummy bear.

But she said yes! I couldn't believe we were actually walking to the center of the gym. At least there were a couple other kids dancing, so we weren't out there alone.

I had ABSOLUTELY no idea how to dance. I just waved my arms around in circles and shuffled my feet from side to side. I tried not to look too hard at Hope, and she was just kind of looking off into other parts of the gym.

The song ended. We all clapped, for some strange reason.

I don't know exactly why I did what I did then. I took Hope's hand!!! It was like a bolt of lightning went up my arm!! And for one whole second, I was TOTALLY HAPPY!!

Then she yanked her hand away and looked at me like I was COMPLETELY NUTS!

I said "Sorry" in a tiny voice probably only dogs can hear.

My face got hot enough to fry an egg on.

Everybody started leaving then. Fine with me! I found

Ronny and Ned. We headed out to the parking lot to look for Ned's dad, who was driving us home.

It took ten minutes to find him, and we were freezing by then. We jumped into the car. Mr. Dorphy turned around.

"Have fun?"

Oh, yeah.

Journal Troubles

I almost lost this journal!!!!
I couldn't find it anywhere.

Not under my bed, or in our car in between cushions, behind furniture, inside my locker, in my book bag, in Haley's room. I checked the lost-and-found box in the school office. I asked Ned and Ronny and Hope.

It VANISHED. I hate when I lose *anything*, but this was a DISASTER!!

I lost it Friday, and it was gone for the whole weekend.

Then Monday, who walks up with my journal? Miles Bumgarten!!

"Hey, you left this at lunch last week. Wanted to make sure you got it back."

I have to say, I was pretty amazed. I would've figured Miles to be the kind to put it in his parents' Weber grill and set it on fire, especially after the dance and my ruining his sweater and everything.

But he was completely chill about it. He even said he was sorry!!

"Hey, sorry about yelling at you at the dance. I was just pretty upset."

"Uh, hey, no problem. I understand. Thanks for getting this back to me!"

Right then, I thought I'd COMPLETELY gotten the wrong idea about Miles.

That didn't last long.

Science was pretty exciting that day. Mr. Moster told us about the Hubble Space Telescope!!! Of course everybody laughed and pointed at me when they heard my name. What else would I expect!!

It turns out the telescope was named after Edwin P. Hubble, who was some heavy-duty astronomy dude. I guess he discovered that the universe was getting bigger. He must have had a monster tape measure!!!!

Then Mr. Moster showed us the coolest pictures taken by the telescope. There were galaxies, and huge gassy explosions called supernovas that looked like colored smoke, and a kratillion zabillion stars.

I nearly forgot the most interesting thing. Mr. Moster said when Edwin Hubble died, he didn't have a funeral, and his wife never said where he was buried!! Maybe we're distant relatives and the family secretly buried him in our backyard somewhere. I'm gonna check.

I was feeling pretty darn good about that whole Hubble thing when my whole life more or less exploded like a supernova.

Ronny came up to me like he'd just seen a dead body and shoved his cell phone in front of my face (FYI, almost everybody but me has a cell phone, too!!).

"Check this out!"

It was a YourFace page. It had my name at the top. It also had a picture of me and said my birthday and where I lived. In the "Whatcha doin'?" box right underneath, it read, "To my buds at the Crumb Middle School," and underneath were little squares of just about every page in my journal. If you clicked on one, you got the whole page, nice and big.

!?!?!?!!?!?!?!?!?!??!?!?!?!??!?!??!?!?!?!??!!?

It was all there. Arnie Stims chasing me in a devil costume. Miss Vanderbeek. Mr. Moster with a squirrel on his head. Throwing up in the pool. Being stuck in the bathroom when everyone else saw the whale.

HOPE!

I darn near fainted and almost lost my lunch. How'd this happen!?!?!? It sure wasn't ME. The laptop Haley

and I use has been at a PC repair shop for a week. The smoke coming out of the keyboard was getting pretty scary, and Mom was afraid it was gonna set the house on fire.

Oh! Of course ... Miles. I was kind of wondering why he was still coming to our Losers' Table. It didn't seem he was that into Hope anymore. A new girl, named Penelope, had moved to our school from Colorado, and he'd been hanging around her a BUNCH!

So looking back, I can see Miles was at our table just to rip off my journal to get back at me for ruining his sweater. I took it out at lunch to write in it last Friday, and he must have grabbed it when I took my tray back to the cafeteria cleanup line. He had my journal for the WHOLE WEEKEND!!!

I was glad it was almost the end of the day. I thought I could get home to figure out what to do, before anyone found out.

But I was already getting weird looks from kids as they passed me in the hall. And Arnie Stims pushed me into a wall, which he pretended was an accident but wasn't.

"Gosh, sorry, Hubble!" He laughed as he walked away.

I had to hand it to Miles. He kept his promises, and did a good job, too! Maybe I wasn't dead, but this was PRETTY DARN CLOSE.

Dark Troubles

In one day, Orville Crumb Middle School became a TOR-TURE CHAMBER, kind of like the ones they used to put in castle basements. Sure, there weren't chains on the walls or metal cages with spikes or that table with ropes where they snap your arms and legs off, and I get a lunch break. But otherwise, pretty much the same thing.

Even lunch got ruined! Our table broke up. Hope went to sit with some girls from the Harry Potter fan club. Ned Dorphy and Phil Zupp are eating with some chess club guys. Mouse Milman somehow got to eat at the girls' soccer team's table. I guess she figured being captain of the badminton team got her in as a jock. WAS SHE KIDDING??

Ronny still ate lunch with me. He's used to being alone, so it's not that hard for him. Still, he's my one ACTUAL friend!

Amazing how many words everyone has for someone like me! I know, 'cause kids say them under their breath when I go by.

Nerd. Dork. Geek. Dweeb. Loser. Drip. Tool. Troll. There are a bunch more that I'll just say are the WORST body parts.

A couple days ago I went into the boys' bathroom to take care of some serious business. I guess someone recognized my special edition Red Sloth sneakers underneath the door. When he left, he flicked out the lights!!!!

There are no windows, so it was COMPLETELY BLACK in there. It took me FIVE WHOLE MINUTES to find the door, I banged my knee on a pipe, and I knocked a trash can over. The kids listening outside in the hall found that pretty hilarious.

Things really went NUTSO last Friday.

I was leaving school using a way I figured out that keeps me TOTALLY out of sight until I get to the bus line. I can get everything out of my locker in (1) twenty seconds or so. Then I (2) duck through the band room, (3) go behind the curtain in the auditorium, (4) shoot into the custodian's supply closet. I wait there for a minute or two until the dismissal bell, then (5) run through the

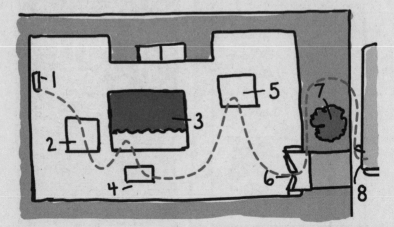

AV studio, (6) leave the school through a delivery door almost nobody uses, and (7) stand between a couple bushes until (8) Mr. Nitz pulls up in Bus 11.

Usually only one or two kids even SEE me.

Bum luck on Friday. Mr. Hintzil opened the door to his supply closet while I was in there, which was PRETTY AWKWARD. The only thing I could think of was to tell him I was doing a science project that used that stinky ammonia stuff and we didn't have any at home. He just looked at me like I was CRAZY, which I totally get. The bell for the buses rang, and I just said, "Gotta run."

That's when Arnie Stims saw me.

"Hey! Look who it is! Orville Crumb's ace reporter!"

Trapped!

Miles Bumgarten came up behind me.

Ambushed!

He grabbed my book bag and pulled out my journal.

"Let's see what we have to say TODAY!"

There was NO WAY he was getting my private book of troubles again. I grabbed it and ran like CRAZY.

I could hear Arnie and Miles behind me. I ran through the band room again and knocked over some music stands and a tuba, which kinda slowed them down for a couple seconds.

I ran back behind the stage curtain, through the AV studio, out the truck delivery door, and down North

Crumb toward
Main Street. I figured
there'd be police or a mailman
or *somebody*.

I looked back. Now it wasn't just Arnie and Miles.
Kincaid Johnson was there, and one or two guys I didn't
even KNOW.

I'm lucky Crumb Hollow's such a dinky town, 'cause
otherwise I'd probably have been TOAST.

I ran to the ComixShop, where I go to buy new Red
Sloth comic books when they come out, which isn't very
often. The owner, Murph (his REAL name is Murphy),
likes me. I guess he knew something was up on account
of I was out of breath and all sweaty.

"Whoa! Where you goin' so fast?!"

"Where can I HIDE?! Some guys are after me!"

Seeing as I'm one of the ComixShop's best customers, Murph of course took my side. He headed for the back of his store and yelled, "C'mon!"

I followed him out the back of the store. Murph opened the smelly dumpster where he throws his trash.

"Get in!" He put his hands down so I could use them for a step.

I looked at him like he was NUTS. But then I heard Arnie yelling "This way!" and decided REAL fast that a few minutes in there was WAY better than getting caught. I took a last gulp of fresh air and went for it.

Just before Murph closed the lid, he whispered, "Hey, for what it's worth, I thought it was the bomb, bro!"

Hiding in a dumpster—
Not as bad as you might think.
Sure, there's cups and wrappers,
And lots of stuff that stinks.

Tuna fish and moldy bread,
Rotten lettuce by my head.
What's this orange junk on my shoe?
Oh, it's just some yogurt goo!

But even in this smelly bin,
I'd like to tell you what:
I'd rather be all safe in here
Than have five guys beat my butt.

Good thing I was in there, 'cause those dudes sounded REAL MAD when they lost me. I heard them just outside the dumpster yelling "Where's the dweeb?" and "Hubble's IN FOR IT!" and a bunch of stuff like that.

I stayed home from school the next day.

And the day after that.

I told Mom I had some stomach thing that was going around and I felt like I was going to throw up. This wasn't EXACTLY lying, because if I went to school I could be punched in the stomach and throw up at ANY time.

That meant I had my neighbor Mrs. Ulanski with me while my folks were at work. Yes, she had Animal Planet on all day, but I'd rather be bored than DEAD!!!

Actually, we were watching *Bad Beasts*, a show about horrible animals that are now TAKING OVER OUR COUNTRY!!!! They showed HUGE pythons that used to only live in China or someplace like that. They got over here somehow, and now people in Florida find them IN THEIR POOLS!! They can swallow your dog or kid brother just like that!

There were these crazy fish called Asian carp that jump out of the water INTO FISHERMEN'S BOATS, give them a good slap in the face, then dive back in!

Even worse were wild pigs (fancy pants name for wild hogs). They're gross, smelly, and nasty, travel in packs, and destroy EVERY SINGLE THING they touch!!

Now that I think of it, kind of like Miles and Arnie and a couple other kids I can think of.

I got a surprise visitor. Ronny showed up in the middle of the day. He was home 'cause he'd had hiccups without stopping for TWO WHOLE DAYS. He said he'd tried everything, including stuff he found on an Internet hiccup website!!

He did three cartwheels with a Jolly Rancher in his mouth.

He ate a Slim Jim and drank a can of Dr Pepper in one minute.

He ate a dill pickle lying on a bed with his head hanging over the side.

Finally, he drank a cup of spicy mustard through a straw. He said that must've worked 'cause he was starting to feel better, but if you ask me, I think they just stopped on their own.

Ronny didn't buy my stomach bug thing for a second. No way.

"How're you feeling?" He had this wiseguy smile, so I knew he didn't think I was sick.

"Oh, y'know, a little better."

"You can't hang out here forever, Hubble. You're gonna have to go back to school."

"I know. Don't know how."

I suggested maybe I could ask Mr. Kretch to see if Crumb Middle School had any sort of student transfer program, where they give you a new name, new clothes, put you with a different family, and change your face with plastic surgery. Ronny thought that had ALL KINDS of problems.

"You'd have to find another family that wants you."

"Maybe I could put an ad on Craigslist or eBay."

"I'm pretty sure that's against the law. And besides, who would you want to look like?"

"I dunno. Justin Bieber?"

"Yeah, well, you don't know. You could ask for Justin Bieber and get Albus Dumbledore."

"Either way, I'd be famous and rich!"

"Oh, yeah, real famous—the kid who looks like Justin Biebledore!"

That cracked us up pretty bad. We got into those giggle fits like you see on MyTube where TV reporters just can't stop themselves from laughing.

Bad news! Ronny's hiccups came back!!! But he said it was worth it.

I remembered an electric sing-along set my folks had in a closet. I pulled out the microphone. "Y'know, I'd have lots of fans! I'd have to give interviews all the time!! Help me practice."

Ronny took the mike. I plugged in the machine and switched it on.

The most horrible sound EVER came out of the speakers.

"YOW! What's that?!"

SCREEOOOOOOOOOOW!!

"Oh, that's feedback." Ronny knows all kinds of electronic and computer stuff.

He looked kinda weird for a couple seconds, like he was somewhere else.

"I think I (hic) know how you can get back (hic) into school."

Whaddyaknow. He did.

HENRY H. HUBBLE
Alias: The Red Sloth
$2 REWARD

I'm Trouble!

If you found this journal under a tree or something and got this far, maybe you already know what happened. It got pretty famous. I guess you could say it went VIRAL!

I admit, that Friday I was pretty nervous getting ready for school! I could barely eat my usual breakfast of toast with peanut butter, CheezWhiz, and raisins.

Haley came down, and first thing she said was "Hey, your journal is really trending on YourFace! Ninety thousand hits! Sweet!!! And thanks for mentioning me, twit! I've gotten about four million Chirps on my phone."

"That's because you have about four million twerps for friends."

"I wouldn't want to be you for ANYTHING! You'll be DEAD MEAT at school."

"Got your wish. Thanks for caring!"

I really don't even remember getting to school.

I climbed up the bus steps. Instead of the usual hoots and wisecracks, there were just stares and silence, which is WAY worse. I headed to my safe seat way in the back.

FYI, I like the last seat, on account of I can look out the back window and wave at drivers behind us. Most of the time they're super mad because the bus stops every fifty yards to pick up another bunch of kids and there's no way to get past us. Half the time the drivers look like they could bite somebody's head off.

But sometimes I get lucky and somebody waves back and smiles. Needless to say, I wasn't waving that day!

I stumbled off the bus and went to my locker. Someone had taped a long strip of toilet paper to it, to make it look like it was coming from inside. Well, that was okay. I was going to fix all that really soon.

The bell for homeroom rang, but instead of going to Mrs. Claster's room, like I always do, I headed in the other direction. It's a pretty big school, so I just barely made it to the office before the bell rang again!

I actually had to get to the AV room, which is right by the office. That's where they make the morning announcements for the WHOLE SCHOOL. Every week they let a different kid do them, so it wasn't strange for me to be in there.

It was my lucky day! Hope Ng was the student announcer that week! She was ALREADY THERE. Shazaam!! This was going WAY better than I thought.

"Um, Henry, what are you doing here?"

"Hey, I was just going by the office, and Mr. Kretch said he needed to give you one more announcement. He said to come get it."

Hope shot out the door, which I locked behind her! No going back now!!!

I'd done announcements one time before, so I knew what to do. I sat behind the mike and turned it on. ALL THE WAY!

Ronny's really smart about science stuff, so I did everything he told me. I put the microphone super close to the box it was plugged into.

SCREEEEEEEEEEEEEEE!!!!!!

The most horrible sound EVER went through every corner of Orville Crumb Middle School. I was live now.

"Hey, everybody! It's me! Henry Harrison Hubble!! Good morning!"

I could already see the shadow of Mr. Kretch at the door of the AV room. He was knocking pretty hard. I knew I didn't have much time.

I kept going. "Hey, I guess you've been reading my journal on MyTube. I heard about all your super feedback!"

I gave everyone a little more feedback of my own. I twirled the mike around the transmitter, just to get some more interesting sounds.

SCREEEEEEEEEUUUUURR-
RROOOOOWWW!

I could hear Mr. Kretch yelling for Mr. Hintzil, who has a key to every lock in the school. I probably had a minute, at most.

"I'm super sorry if anything I wrote hurt anybody's feelings. But guess what? Miles Bumgarten swiped my journal from me during lunch when I wasn't looking. And then he put it on YourFace without asking me or anything. That's stealing, right? And when you think of it, is there anything worse than swiping someone's personal thoughts and spreading them around for the whole world to look at?!

"So I just want to say that whatever I put in my journal, my thoughts are MY BUSINESS! NOT MILES'S, AND NOT YOURS!!!"

The lock clicked.

"GOTTA RUN! Have a wonderful day!"

I finished up with one sonic boom.

143

SCREEEEEEEEUUUUURR-RREEEOOOOUUOOORRROOOOOWWW!

Phillip told me later that last one broke a couple test tubes in the science lab.

I got up. Mr. Hintzil and Mr. Kretch were at the door.

"Oh, hi, Mr. Hintzil! Hi, Mr. Kretch!"

But Mr. Kretch had his hands over his ears, and Mr. Hintzil was just shaking his head back and forth, like a dog that has a bug in its ear!

I went out into the hall. Hope was there, with her

hands still over her ears. But she gave me a REALLY big smile.

Mr. Kretch held up his hand and curled his finger at me a couple times to signal me to come to his office.

 I knew he was going to call my folks. I figured I'd probably be suspended again. But I didn't care.

Ronny Bartz was in Miles Bumgarten's homeroom. I knew that he recorded the WHOLE THING with his phone while Miles hid his face behind a book.

And I knew it was already posted on MyTube.

Things got pretty nuts after that. Mom and Dad had to come get me, but not before having a BIG powwow with Mr. Kretch, Mrs. Claster, and Mrs. Havlocker, the school guidance counselor! Like *I* was the one who was crazy!

They weren't mad, exactly, but they said I had below-average social skills. I think they're wrong. As far as I can tell, I don't have any social skills whatsoever.

Sure, I had to say I was sorry for breaking everyone's eardrums (Mr. Hintzil was out the next day with a super bad headache). And I had to pay for the test tubes that broke in the science lab. (TWELVE WHOLE DOLLARS!!! Now I only have $27 left in my shoe box!)

But Mrs. Havlocker said I had good reasons for doing what I did, even if she didn't like my way of handling everything. So they ended up not suspending me.

WHEW!!

I'm writing this at two o'clock in the morning. I can't believe I'm still awake! My brain's buzzin' with everything that happened over the past couple days!

We spent the whole weekend in New York visiting my aunt Judith and her bunions. Mom finally explained that bunions are these big bumps that stick out of your feet that hurt a lot. So I guess that explains why Aunt Judith's always such a GRUMP. And why she wears the worst shoes in America!!

First thing Monday morning Ronny called me.

"Hey, Hubble! You're like some kind of dweeb hero! The video from last Friday has gotten 650,000 Thumz-Ups!"

"Geez! Is that good?"

"Hmmm. Lemme think.... DUUU-UUUH!"

Even before my school bus pulled into the parking lot, I could tell things were INSANE! There was a news truck with one of those big dish thingies sticking up in the air.

I saw Mr. Kretch and Mrs. Claster being interviewed by some reporter lady.

I got closer to hear what the heck was going on. I heard Mr. Kretch say, "Well, we've found Henry to be a very resourceful and unusual boy who marches to his own drummer."

"More like a guy playing bongos!" said Mrs. Claster.

Somebody yelled, "Oh! There he is!!"

The reporter came up to ME!

"Here's the man of the hour, Henry Hubble! Do you know that your school announcement has been viewed almost a million times on My-Tube since Friday?"

"Um, no. I was with my family visiting my aunt Judith in New York. She has bunions."

That stopped the reporter lady for a second or two.

"Well, young man, let me tell you something. You really struck a chord with a lot of kids out there who feel a real connection to what you've been through and LOVE what you told your classmates."

"Wow. That's great, I guess."

"You bet it's great! Is there anything else you'd like to tell all the folks watching you now?"

I had to think about that REAL hard.

"I guess I'd like to say that a lot of people don't pay near enough attention to President William Henry—"

That's as far as I got, 'cause Mrs. Claster kind of grabbed my arm and announced that school was starting any minute.

I have to say, I was pretty popular for a while. Some kid I never met before even asked me for an autograph!

Dad bought Haley and me a new laptop, 'cause it turned out the old one was pretty much toast. So now I could check my new YourFace page. I got ThumbzUps from all over, even from Hong Kong and Ireland and BRAZIL!

I even got a YourFace message from some kid in Buffalo, New York, who's somehow a relative of Millard Fillmore, the thirteenth president of the United States. So things are pretty exciting!

Oh, almost forgot!! I'm going to a movie with Hope! She has a thing for dogs, so we're going to see the next Beverly Hills Chihuahua movie (ugh!). But who cares!!

I made it to the end of the journal.

But in case I leave this someplace tomorrow, like the

ComixShop or the mall, thanks ahead of time for getting it back to me!!

P.S. Went to Walmart today. Bought a new journal. Now I only have $12!

Today at lunch, holding my fork,
Thinkin' 'bout my past life as a dork.
Yet there I was, next to old friends.
That's how my first journal ends.
Instead of troubles, at last some good news!
That's all for now. I gotta snooze!

Acknowledgments

Many thanks to Beth Hagel for her kid-savvy editing, to my family for enduring Henry's early chapters, and to Sammi's fourth-grade class at Groveland Elementary School for being willing subjects in my consumer testing of Henry Hubble's language concerns. Special thanks to Michelle Poploff, my editor at Delacorte Press, and to Deborah Warren and Rubin Pfeffer, the illustrious duo at East West Literary Agency.

YEARLING

Turning children into readers for more than fifty years.

**Classic and award-winning literature for every shelf.
How many have you checked out?**

**Find the perfect book, play games,
and meet favorite authors at RandomHouseKids.com!**